Dangerous potatoes

Acknowledgements

To my wife Ann, thank you for saving my life.

My eldest daughter Lula, the original Monkeyman.

My boys and girls Jake, Callum, Olivia and Willow
for listening in wide eyed amazement.

My sister Jackie and my nephews Sean and Simon
for Easter egg hunts in Bluebell wood, (In the day time of course).

Mark, Joanne, Samuel and Toby for help with the finer details.

Special thanks to Roger King for pointing out my over use of the lowly comma
and Sarah Kershaw for relighting the fire

This book is born out of bedtime stories.

Never stop telling them.

Cover colouring and layout Steve Cripps

Editing and proof reading Mark Webb and Adrienne Staniford

Published by Diverze Publishing - www.diverze-publishing.com

First Edition - Printed 2012 in Great Britain by Diverze Print - www.diverze-print.com

Foreword

Some children don't like soggy cabbage, smelly sprouts or bitter broccoli but, of course, everyone loves potatoes. They are just delicious chipped, roasted, mashed or fried. Unless, they happen to be Dangerous Potatoes! (Solanum Tuberosum Periculosum.)

"How can a potato be dangerous?" I hear you ask. Well, if you've never seen a Dangerous Potato you're very lucky. The children in this book weren't quite so lucky! But, you'll have to read the stories to find out just how dangerous potatoes can be!

Oh, but before you get started there's one more thing you need to know about Dangerous Potatoes. They can change nature around themselves. They can turn normal things into unusual things, because they are freaks of the vegetable world. And beware. Even listening to stories about Dangerous Potatoes can make strange things happen to you. However, the truth is, Dangerous Potatoes just want to be left alone and it's only when people bother them that problems begin. But isn't all of nature like that?!!!

The problems were only just about to begin for the children who lived in a strange sleepy little town, but for your own safety it's best you don't know where it is. No, I'm not going to tell you just incase you are tempted to go there and search for Dangerous Potatoes yourself. That would be asking for trouble. What I will say is it's a small picturesque little English town with wiggly, winding roads that amble between pretty, well-kept gardens. It's a bit of an old-fashioned place with lots of things left over from the olden days... Days which your mummy and daddy may remember. So if anything seems very old and strange in this book, just ask your parents.

Meanwhile here's a map of the town to get you started.

N
Timmy Trolley Bus' House
School
Bluebell Wood
Dangerous Potatoes
Beware.
Wiggley Windey Road
Monkeyman's Garage
Squinkle's house
Sweet shop
Wika Waka's house
Police Station. Jail

Story Twelve

Cluck Cluck

Chapter 1

Cluck Cluck

It was early in the morning and the three friends were fast asleep upstairs on Monkeyman's floor. Downstairs in the garage, the mummy hen started to cluck cluck noisily. It wasn't long before everyone was wiping the sleep from their eyes.

"What time is it?" yawned Squinkle.

"Time to get up," sighed Monkeyman. "We've got work to do."

Stumbling downstairs and pulling a pink cardigan on, Monkeyman started to pour fresh birdseed into a little tray and feed it to the fluffy chicken and the mummy hen.

"Yeah, that's right!" said Wika Waka, following her into the garage. "We've got to get my trainers back from Bluebell Wood."

"That as well," said Monkeyman matter-of-factly.

"What do you mean, 'that as well?' What else do we have to do today?" asked Wika Waka.

"If we're ever going to understand anything about the Dangerous Potatoes, we've got to collect some samples and bring them back here for tests," she said, equally matter-of-factly.

"You mean...Invite the Dangerous Potatoes round?" asked Squinkle in disbelief.

"Nope! Catch them. Lots of them," replied Monkeyman.

"And bring them back here?" asked Wika Waka.

"You bet!" said Monkeyman.

"Don't you think that's just a little bit dangerous?" asked Wika Waka.

"And just a little bit mad?" asked Squinkle.

"Look! We can either stay away from Bluebell Wood because we're frightened of them, or we can catch some and try to understand them," lectured Monkeyman.

"I know which *I* prefer to do," Squinkle exclaimed. "Just leave them alone."

Wika Waka took a deep breath. "Actually, I think Monkeyman's right," he said. "We've spent too long living in fear of the Dangerous Potatoes. It's time we found out just what makes them so dangerous and so scary........... I'm with you Monkeyman."

"Good," said Monkeyman.

"Mad! You've both gone mad. Totally Mad! And I'm supposed to be the silly one," sniffed Squinkle walking off in a huff.

"Come on," said Monkeyman to Wika Waka, "You can help me get the stuff ready."

The little fluffy chicken and the mummy hen pecked happily away at the birdseed while Monkeyman and Wika Waka crashed and bashed away in the background.

"Three pairs of metal pants," she said, banging them down on the table.

"Some oven gloves and a sack," added Wika waka.

"Some tongs," said Monkeyman.

"That's all we need for now," said Monkeyman, slightly out of breath.

"Mad! Totally mad," muttered Squinkle in disbelief.

"Right, buckle up! We're going potato hunting," said Monkeyman.

Chapter 2

"A huntin' we will go"

Of course Squinkle didn't sulk for long. In the end he shrugged his shoulders and followed them. The three children approached Bluebell Wood in a clatter of metal pants and with their assorted equipment in tow. "It is daytime you know," said Squinkle hoping they would all give up and go home. "Dangerous Potatoes don't come out during the day. So why are we wearing these ridiculous metal pants?"

"We've got to catch some remember?" snapped Monkeyman.

"But first let's find my trainers," said Wika Waka.

It was a lovely sunny day and the trees swayed gently in the breeze. The bluebells shimmered amongst the grass and the children felt safe as they wandered through the wood. "Found 'em!" shouted Wika Waka. "Right where we left 'em, up a tree." He pointed to the shoes that hung upside down from a big branch. Pulling out his catapult he fired a big stone and knocked both the training shoes down with one shot. "Bullseye!" he shouted, jumping up and down excitedly. Quickly, he ran and strapped on the shoes.

"That's better. I'm ready to catch Dangerous Potatoes now," he grinned.

"Good. Come on then," giggled Monkeyman.

"I still think you're both mad, totally mad," sighed Squinkle.

Monkeyman brandished a big dessert spoon in her left hand, and a pair of wooden wash tongs in her oven-gloved right hand. Slowly, quietly, and very very carefully, she crept over the carpet of bluebells, looking down for a place to start digging.

"Sssssshhhhh," she whispered to the boys as they clattered clumsily behind her. "I think there's some sleeping under our feet," she added, pointing down.

"We're all going to get bitten," whimpered Squinkle.

Monkeyman pulled out a doctor's stethoscope, held it to the ground and listened intently. The sound of loud shuddering snores could be heard. "Yes, they're asleep alright," she confirmed. "Wika Waka, you hold the sack open. And whatever happens, ***don't panic***. Do you understand?"

"Yes. Don't panic," repeated Wika Waka.

"Do you understand Squinkle?" asked Monkeyman.

"Yes," replied Squinkle. "Don't pic-nic."

Monkeyman rolled her eyes.

Slowly she started to dig away at the soft brown earth between the bluebells with her big dessert spoon. Gently she uncovered the first sleeping, snoring Dangerous Potato. Squinkle shivered in fear. Wika Waka elbowed him while Monkeyman reached down with the wash tongs and lifted it very gently. "Open the sack," she muttered to Wika Waka, then she dropped the sleeping Dangerous Potato inside.

"Can we go now?" whimpered Squinkle.

"No. We need a lot more than that," answered Monkeyman, stooping once again to dig. Slowly she uncovered five more snoring potatoes and one by one, lifted them up to the sack. But suddenly, the sixth potato opened its yellow beady eyes and quickly started to gnash its teeth.

"DON'T PANIC! DON'T PANIC!" screamed Squinkle at the top of his voice.

Chapter 3

PANIC!

Suddenly all the other potatoes were awake and shook themselves free from beneath the remaining earth. Monkeyman snatched at them with the tongs and managed to sling three more into the sack, without getting bitten. But another sprang up from the ground and tried to bite her on the bottom, breaking its teeth on her metal pants.

"DON'T PANIC! DON'T PANIC! DON'T PANIC!" screamed Squinkle hysterically, running round in circles with his arms in the air.

"Shut up Squinkle!" shouted Monkeyman, as she wrestled with an enormous angry Dangerous Potato. Wika Waka wanted to help but was too busy holding down the sack, which was now full of angry bouncing potatoes. Monkeyman let out a scream as one bit through her oven glove. "Aaaaaaaaahhhhhhh," she yelled. She hit it very hard on the head with the spoon until it fell off into the sack.

"DON'T PANIC! DON'T PANIC! DON'T PANIC!" yelled Squinkle in blind terror.

"Calm down Squinkle," shouted Wika Waka, still wrestling with the jumping sack. Monkeyman fell back, reeling from the force of a potato that she caught mid-flight with her tongs, its teeth bared and barking at her only inches from her face. Somehow Wika Waka managed to grab the Dangerous Potato with the sack and pull it off her, as thousands of beady eyes blinked open from beneath the soil. "Let's get out of here!" shouted Monkeyman.

"BUT DON'T PANIC! DON'T PANIC! DON'T PANIC!" panted Squinkle, running faster than all of them.

The potatoes were gaining on Wika Waka and Monkeyman, when Wika Waka shouted out... "Piggyback Monkeyman!"

Monkeyman instantly jumped onto Wika Waka's back as he kicked the special button on the side of his training shoes. Suddenly they started to buzz and whirr and, in a blaze of lights and flashes, the training shoes propelled the two children past Squinkle and out of the trees to safety.

Squinkle arrived shortly behind them, pursued right to the edge of Bluebell Wood by thousands of bouncing Dangerous Potatoes.

"DON'T PANIC! DON'T PANIC! DON'T PANIC!" he groaned breathlessly, as he fell to the ground exhausted.

The three children stood and watched as the Dangerous Potatoes howled and barked at the edge of the wood, and then sank back under the ground to sleep. Slowly the sack in Wika Waka's hand also stopped wriggling. The sound of loud snoring could be heard once more as the potatoes fell asleep in the darkness of the sack.

"Why can't you just play with dolls like other girls?" snapped Squinkle to Monkeyman.

Monkeyman pulled off her oven glove and looked down at her bleeding hand.

Chapter 4

Normal Girl

The fluffy chicken and mummy hen were delighted to see the children when they arrived back at Monkeyman's Garage. They clucked and cheeped with excitement. But the children were too busy to take any notice. They had work to do. Dangerous work. Monkeyman went over to a big tank with toughened glass sides and lifted the lid. "OK," she said. "Tip them in Wika Waka."

Wika Waka lifted the sack up to the tank and emptied the Dangerous Potatoes into it. As they fell out of the sack, their eyes blinked open in surprise. Soon they were all jumping up and down angrily, staring back defiantly at their captors.

Monkeyman locked the lid just before one could bite her finger. "What makes them so fierce?" asked Wika Waka.

"Let's find out," said Monkeyman. Reaching cautiously in with her glove and tongs she caught one of the potatoes. Instantly three others grabbed onto her glove with their teeth and wouldn't let go. She shook her hand but they held on like limpets. Reaching over with her free hand she picked up an electric cattle prod. (You wouldn't believe the gadgets you would find in Monkeyman's garage!) Quickly she jabbed it into the three potatoes. Electric sparks buzzed and crackled as they tumbled off one by one, smelling a bit like chips.

"Now let's see what makes them tick shall we?" she asked, carefully lowering the Dangerous Potato into a vice and then tightened it into place. The Dangerous

Potato stretched and swelled, but try as it might, it couldn't get free from the tight grip. Then it got angrier and angrier, gnashing its teeth and trying to bite anything that came near it.

The little fluffy chicken ran and hid under its mummy's feathers and poked its tiny beak out to see what would happen next. The mummy hen clucked nervously.

"First let's see what happens when they get wet," said Monkeyman. Slowly she lifted a glass of water and dripped a little onto the Dangerous Potato. SHPLANG!!!!!!!!!!!! Instantly the potato exploded, showering everyone in mash.

The little fluffy chicken disappeared from sight under its mummy's feathers and started cheeping loudly.

"That I did not expect!" said Monkeyman as she wiped mashed potato out of her eyes.

"Me neither," said Wika Waka doing the same.

"We're all going to die!" moaned Squinkle squinting through his potato-spattered glasses.

"Let's try another one," said Wika Waka clapping his hands together in excitement.

"OK," said Monkeyman and reached in to pull out another of the vicious potatoes.

Again, she carefully locked it in the vice and picked up a hair drier. "Now let's see what happens when they get hot?" Slowly she turned up the heat on the hair drier and held it in front of the growling Dangerous Potato. To their amazement, even as it snarled and barked at them, it slowly started to melt! It slithered and dripped onto the floor of the garage and formed a little puddle of goo.

Fluffy chicken and mummy hen both looked on fascinated and a little relieved.

"What is that?" asked Monkeyman, as Squinkle and Wika Waka gathered around the strange mess on the floor. To their amazement it was oozing and bulging in the middle as if it were still alive. Squinkle reached down to touch it but Monkeyman shouted out............ "DON'T TOUCH IT!"

Too late. The gooey mess flew up and wrapped itself around Squinkle's hand. He snatched his hand back in surprise.

"It might be dangerous like that," she warned.

"It won't come off!" he complained shaking his hand frantically.

"Cover it with this towel," said Monkeyman, already thinking of the next experiment.

"We'll get it off later."

What next?" asked Wika Waka. "There're still loads of potatoes left."

"Let's try high voltage electricity," suggested Monkeyman, giggling to herself.

"OK," laughed Wika Waka................

Squinkle just looked at his hand.

Chapter 5

DANGER High Voltage

Monkeyman reached into the glass tank and pulled out a particularly mean and nasty Dangerous Potato. She gripped the tongs tightly, with both hands this time to make sure it didn't shake itself free and bite someone. "OK. Open the vice wider, this one's a biggy!" Wika Waka quickly unwound the vice while Monkeyman wrestled the potato into position. It snarled and growled at all of them with fierce angry eyes and white gnashing teeth. "Don't you dare drop it," sniffled Squinkle still nursing his hand, which was now starting to hurt him.

Fluffy chicken hid deeper in mummy hen's feathers and shivered in fear.

What happened next is very dangerous and should not be tried by any of you reading this book!

"Right, where are my jump leads?" muttered Monkeyman to herself. Reaching over she lifted some red and black electric cables in either hand and touched the two ends together. Instantly they arced and sent orange sparks flashing across the garage. "OK. Here we go then," she said bracing herself. Everyone looked on transfixed as Monkeyman brought the two cables down on either side of the Dangerous Potato's head. Instantly it made a low growling noise and shuddered in the dancing blue electric current. The growl got louder and louder until, to everyone's amazement, the Dangerous Potato shot out of the vice like a bullet and bounced all over the garage.

"Get down!" shouted Monkeyman as it smashed and shattered everything in its path. It smashed holes in the ceiling and flew straight through a wooden table. It smashed more holes in the floor and eventually knocked over the glass tank, releasing the other Dangerous Potatoes.

"OH NO!" shouted Squinkle. *"THEY'RE FREE.* ***PANIC!****"*

Finally the electrified potato smashed through the window and disappeared quickly out of view. Meanwhile Monkeyman and Wika Waka grabbed fluffy chicken and mummy hen and turned some tables over to hide behind. The remaining potatoes were really mad and they knew where the children were hiding. Tearing at the wood with their razor sharp teeth, they growled and chewed their way through the tables while the children huddled helplessly in a corner. They watched as beady eyes started to emerge through the wood and spat sawdust at them. One by one the Dangerous Potatoes chomped and inched closer.

Monkeyman held her breath. Wika Waka closed his eyes. Squinkle whimpered and trembled and fluffy chicken hid under mummy hen's feathers.

Suddenly, from far away in the distance, there came a strange eerie noise. Like someone sounding an evil trumpet on a foggy night.

All the Dangerous Potatoes stopped and turned in the direction of the sound. One by one, without looking back, they marched out through the broken window.

"What happened? Why aren't we dead?" asked Squinkle looking at his gooey hand.

"Bluebell Wood," said Monkeyman as she walked over to the broken window and looked out. "They're being called home to Bluebell Wood."

Wika Waka came and stood next to Monkeyman and watched as the Dangerous Potatoes bounced off into the distance.

"It's getting dark now. And they know where we live," said Wika Waka grimly.

"Yes! And we know what they're afraid of," said Monkeyman lifting up the hair drier and a jug of water.

Wika Waka turned round then froze to the spot. "Maybe we do, but I think we've got a bigger problem right now," he said. Monkeyman turned round and they both stared at Squinkle. He was shivering, looking mean and holding out his arm... which now had nine Dangerous Potatoes growing all over it.

The End